RACHEL PARKER,
KINDERGARTEN SHOW-OFF

For E.M.M., H.R.M., and J.R.M.
Ann Martin

To my mother and father
Nancy Poydar

Text copyright © 1992 by Ann M. Martin
Illustrations copyright © 1992 by Nancy Poydar
Printed in the United States of America
All rights reserved
Library of Congress Cataloging-in-Publication Data
Martin, Ann M., 1955-
    Rachel Parker, kindergarten show-off / by Ann M. Martin ;
illustrated by Nancy Poydar. — 1st ed.
        p.   cm.
    Summary: Five-year-old Olivia's new neighbor Rachel is in her
kindergarten class, and they must overcome feelings of jealousy
and competitiveness to be friends.
    ISBN 0-8234-0935-X
    [1. Friendship—Fiction. 2. Kindergarten—Fiction. 3. Schools—
Fiction.] I. Poydar, Nancy, ill. II. Title.
PZ7.M3567585Rac   1992   91-25793   CIP   AC
[E]—dc20
    ISBN 0-8234-1067-6 (pbk.)

RACHEL PARKER, KINDERGARTEN SHOW-OFF

BY ANN MARTIN

ILLUSTRATED BY NANCY POYDAR

HOLIDAY HOUSE / NEW YORK

I am Olivia. I am five years old. I go to kindergarten. I am very good at kindergarten.
Everyone says so.

My teacher has long hair. Also a long name. Her name is Mrs. Beejorgenhoosen. She lets us call her Mrs. Bee. I love my teacher.

This is my family: me, Mommy, Daddy.
I do not have any brothers or sisters.

But I have a cat. Her name is Rosie. Rosie is my
very best friend. Except for Mrs. Bee. And except for
Mommy. And except for Daddy.

Hop, hop, hop. I am hopping
around my room. I leap onto my bed.
I jump on the bed for a while.

"Olivia?" calls Mommy. "Are
you jumping on your bed?"
"Not anymore!" I yell back.

I look out the window. I see
something interesting. A moving van is
parked in front of the house next door.
That house has been empty forever.

I run out of my room.
I clatter downstairs.

"Who's that?" says
Mommy.
"It's me, Olivia!" I reply.
"Guess what! There's a
moving van next door."
"Good," says Mommy.
"New neighbors. Maybe a
girl just your age will move
in."
"Maybe," I answer.

I am in school. I have big news. "Mrs. Bee? Oh, Mrs. Bee! I have something to share with the class," I say.

Mrs. Bee smiles. "Can you save it for sharing time, Olivia?"

"I hope so."

In sharing time we sit on the floor in a circle.

"Who has something to share?" asks Mrs. Bee.

I shoot my hand in the air.

"Olivia?" says Mrs. Bee.

I stand up. "We are getting new neighbors,"
I announce.
    I sit down.
    "When?" asks Molly.
    I stand up again. "Tomorrow," I tell her.
    I sit down.
    "Any kids?" asks Lou.
    I stand up again. "I don't know,"
I tell him. Before I sit down again,
I say, "Any more questions?"
There are no more questions, so I sit down.
    I love sharing time.

Jump, jump, jump.

I am jumping on my bed. Also, I am looking out my
window. I see a car pull into the driveway next door.

I leap off the bed.
I run out of my room.
I clatter downstairs.

"Who's that?" says Mommy.
"It's me, Olivia!" I reply.
"Guess what. The new
people are moving in!
I'm going to watch."

I stand in our driveway. I lean on the fence. I look next door.

A mommy and a daddy and a granddaddy are walking to the house. The mommy is carrying a baby. Behind the granddaddy is a girl.

I think she might be about five years old.

The girl sees me. She runs to the fence.

"Hi!" she says. "I am Rachel Elizabeth Parker."

"You have *two* first names?" I reply. (I only have one.)

"Yes. But you can call me Rachel," says Rachel Elizabeth Parker. "I am five. I am going to go to kindergarten. I will have a new teacher. Her name is Mrs. Beejorgenhoosen."

"I think you are in my class," I say.

"Goody!" says Rachel. "What's your name?"

"Olivia."

"Do you like kindergarten?"

"I *love* kindergarten. I can already read. And I can write stories. No one else in my class can read or write yet."

"I can read and write," says Rachel.

Uh-oh.

In school the next day, Mrs. Bee says,
"Boys and girls, we have
a new student. Her name is Rachel Parker."

Rachel is standing at the front of my
kindergarten room. Mrs. Bee's arm
is around her.

I will try to be nice to Rachel.

I raise my hand. "I know Rachel," I say.
"She moved next door to me.
She has two first names.
Rachel Elizabeth."

Rachel smiles at me. I smile back.

Mrs. Bee shows Rachel to a desk. Rachel's desk
is next to mine.

At storytime, Rachel says, "Oh, Mrs. Bee! Oh, Mrs. Bee! I know how to read!"

"Wonderful," says Mrs. Bee. "Would you like to read to your new class today?"

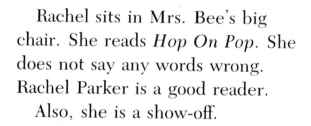

Rachel sits in Mrs. Bee's big chair. She reads *Hop On Pop*. She does not say any words wrong. Rachel Parker is a good reader. Also, she is a show-off.

"Oh, Mrs. Bee! Oh, Mrs. Bee!" I say. "I could read *Hop On Pop* when I was four. I can read much harder books now that I am five."

"I can too," says Rachel. "*Hop On Pop* is easy for me."

I think about sticking my tongue out at Rachel. I decide not to.

When school is over, Mrs. Bee says, "Rachel, I am glad you are in our class."

And Rachel says to me, "Olivia, can you come over and play?"

"Maybe," I answer.

Mommy says I should play with Rachel. She says, "Rachel is new here. It would be nice if you went to her house."

Ding-dong. I ring Rachel's doorbell.

"Hi," says Rachel.

"Hi," I say. "I am here to play."

Rachel's house is a mess.
There is stuff everywhere.
Nothing is put away yet.

Rachel likes the mess. "It is good for hide-and-seek," she says.

I meet Lily. Lily is Rachel's
baby sister. I tickle Lily's toes.
"Hi, Lily! Hi, Lily!" I say. Lily
smiles at me.

I meet Poppa. Poppa is Rachel's
granddaddy. "I hope you like
candy," he says. He gives me a
root beer barrel and a peppermint.

"I will show you my room," Rachel says.
We run upstairs.
"This is it. I share it with Lily."
"I would not want a crib in *my* room," I say.
"I like the crib."
"The diaper pail smells."
"I like the diaper pail."
That cannot be true.

"Let's play house," says Rachel. "You be the daddy."

"No. Let's put on a play."

"No. Let's put on a puppet show. I have a puppet theater."

Rachel Parker has a puppet theater?
And a baby sister?
And a grandfather who gives out candy?
And two first names?

"I have to go home now," I say.
"Good-bye."

Mommy says I should invite Rachel Elizabeth Parker to my house. She says, "Rachel invited you. Now you should invite Rachel over." So I do.

I watch for Rachel out my window. Here she comes.

Rachel and I jump on my bed for a while.

"Olivia!" calls Mommy. "Are you jumping on your bed?"

"Not anymore!" I yell back.

Rachel and I leap onto the floor.

"Do you share your room with anyone?" Rachel
asks me.

"No," I answer proudly. "It is all mine."

"Don't you have any brothers or sisters?"

"I have a cat," I tell Rachel. "Her name is Rosie. She
knows what *dinner* means. And also what *outside* means.
And what *birdie* means. When I say 'birdie,' she runs to
the window to look for one."

"Oh," says Rachel. "Lily is very smart, too. She knows
some words. Plus, she can almost walk. And she is not
even a year old yet."

I frown. "Rosie could walk when she was a *month* old."

Now Rachel frowns. "Have you ever moved?" she asks.
"*I* have moved two times."

I have not moved. Not once. So I say, "No. But I have
an uncle who lives in Texas. He sent me a pair of real
cowgirl boots. And a cowgirl hat."

"Well, I am writing a story about a cowgirl," says Rachel.

"I am writing a book," I say.

"I wrote a book last year," says Rachel. "When I was
four."

That cannot be true. Rachel Parker is an enormous
show-off.

"I think I hear your mother calling," I tell Rachel.

"Me, too," she answers. "I have to go home now.
Good-bye."

Everybody likes Rachel. My mommy and daddy like
her. "What a nice friend she is," they say. Mrs. Bee likes
Rachel. Molly and Lou and the other kids in school like
Rachel.

On the playground I swing by myself. Back and forth,
back and forth. I do not feel like playing with anybody.

I look all around. I watch the other kids.

Uh-oh. Here comes Rachel.

"Can I swing with you?" she asks.

"I don't care."

Rachel climbs into the swing next to mine. She pumps her legs. She can swing very high.

So can I. I pump my legs, too. "I am higher than you!" I call to Rachel.

Rachel pumps harder. "Now I am higher than you!" she cries.

"Show-off!" I shout.

"Show-off!" Rachel shouts back.

I drag my feet to stop my swing. Rachel stops, too.

"Show-off!" I say again. "Just leave me alone, Rachel Parker."

"You know what?" Rachel yells. "You are very mean, Olivia."

"So what."

"So I do not want to be your friend."
"Good!" I say. "I do not want you to be
my friend either."
I run away from Rachel.
(I feel like I might cry.)

I look out my window. I
watch Rachel. She is playing
with Lily. "Peek-a-boo!"
cries Rachel. Lily laughs.

I sit on my bed. I cross
my arms. I am still mad at
Rachel.
  Also, I am bored.

I run out of my room.
I clatter downstairs.

"Who's that?" says Mommy.
"It's just me, Olivia," I reply.

"Mommy, can we get a baby, please? I want a
brother or a sister. Either one. Rachel has a sister.
She always has a friend to play with. I bet she is
never lonely."

"Are you lonely?" Mommy asks.
"Who, me?" I say. "No. Well, maybe.
Maybe a little."
"Why don't you play with Rachel?"
"No."

I do not tell Mommy about our fight. Instead, I go back to my room. I look for a book. I look for *Little Bear*. I read it two times.

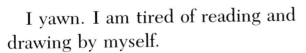

Then I look for my paper. I make up a story about two girls who have a fight. I draw a picture of the fight.

I yawn. I am tired of reading and drawing by myself.

I look out my window again. I watch Rachel give Lily a ride in the stroller.

At school we have sharing time. Rachel and I sit far
apart. We can see each other. I cross my eyes at Rachel.
She sticks her tongue out at me.

"Who has something to share?" asks Mrs. Bee.

Rachel raises her hand.
"We are going to get a cat,"
she says.

I raise my hand.
"*We* already have a cat," I say.

"That's enough, girls," says
Mrs. Bee.

I shrug my shoulders.

After sharing, Mrs. Bee says, "Class, today you will have two new teachers. Their names are Olivia and Rachel. They will read to you."

Mrs. Bee sits on the floor. She waits for Rachel and me to choose a book. Then we fight over Mrs. Bee's big chair. Guess what—we can fit in it together.

Rachel begins to read to our class. She reads the first page of the book.

I read the second page.

Uh-oh. Here is a word I do not know. "Mrs. Bee?" I say.

"Mrs. Bee?" my teacher repeats. "Who is that? I do not know any Mrs. Bee. My new name is Alice, and I cannot read yet."

"Oh." I skip over the word. Now the story does not make sense.

Rachel whispers something to me. "It's *jacket*," she says. "That word is *jacket*."

"Thank you," I reply.

On the next page, Rachel gets stuck on a word. So I whisper it to her.

"Thank you," she replies.

We read the story to the end. When we finish, I smile at Rachel. Maybe she is not such a show-off. Then I say, "Can you come over after school?"

At my house, Rachel and I make a train out of chairs. We pretend to take a trip to Italy.

Then we tie a bonnet on Rosie. We pretend she is our baby.

After that, we pretend we are teachers again.

I read *Little Bear* to Rachel. She reads *The Snowy Day* to me.

"Rachel!" calls Mommy. "Your grandfather wants you to come home now."

"Okay!" Rachel answers. "Olivia, tomorrow you can come to my house."

"And the next day, you can come here again," I say.

"Good-bye, Olivia. I will see you tomorrow."
"Good-bye, Rachel Elizabeth Parker. I am glad you are my friend."